Life In, Life Out

by

Avital Gad-Cykman

Matter Press
Wynnewood, Pennsylvania

Life In, Life Out
Copyright © 2014
Published by Matter Press
First Matter Press Edition, 2014

Thank you to the editors of the following publications
where some of these fictions first appeared, some in
alternate versions: "Major Chaos" in *The Flash: A Flash
Fiction Anthology;* "Once a Month We Play" in *Prism
International;* "Crystal and Gold" in *NOÖ Journal;* "Nature"
in *3:AM;* "Boxing" in *Flash: The International Short-Short
Story Magazine;* "Running Away Diary" in *Portland Magazine
& Dragons with Cancer Anthology* ; "String Theory" in *The
Journal of Compressed Creative Arts;* "Get Down To It" in
NANO Fiction; "Soap" in *The Salt River Review;* "Out
of Order" in *Gigantic;* "Somewhere Station" in *Eclectica;*
"The Spirit of His Will" in *Absinthe Review;* "Wings" in
Pindeldyboz; "Sudden Changes" in *Happy* and *Pig Iron Malt,
Web Del Sol;* "The Future of Color" & "Perfect for This
World" in *Salon;* "Tiny Love Stories" in *Dispatch;* "Unless"
in *Corium Magazine;* "Bison" in *Los Angeles Review;* "Fire.
Water." in *Smokelong Quarterly* & W.W. Norton's *Flash Fiction
International Anthology;* "A Narrow Bridge" in *Every Writer
Resource;* and "About My Life Length" in *Quick Fiction.*

Photography and cover design by Vered Navon.

ISBN 978-0-9837928-9-5

Matter Press
P.O. Box 704
Wynnewood, PA 19096

Life In, Life Out

CONTENTS

One: Sudden Changes

Two: Minute Life Length

One:

SUDDEN CHANGES

MAJOR CHAOS

Major Chaos came here one of those hot days. I was washing the floor, wearing old clothes, when he knocked on my door. Since I don't have many visits, I let him in. At first, he seemed like a paratrooper, but upon reflection I realized he was a big green frog. It may sound peculiar, but believe me: a man who jumps from airplanes can't look any better than that.

He said he had seen my name downstairs and liked the sound of it. I thought it strange to visit a woman because of her name, but I said nothing. Everyone has his reasons. Remembering my neighbor, arrested while trying to stab another man, I decided that his visit was neither a crime, nor as weird as it might seem.

Since Major Chaos had made it all the way down from the sky to the earth, he was very hungry. I noticed the interest with which he glanced at the oranges in the kitchen. I threw him one, and he, smiling, caught it with one hand while grabbing a chair with the other. I didn't know what to do with the bucket, full of soapy water, so I kicked it and the water washed the floor. Major Chaos pulled a camera out of his pocket and took a picture of the wet floor. I thought he might take one of me too, so I arranged my clothes, but he put the camera away.

While he sliced the orange, I stared at his froggy face. In his way he was attractive. But not in mine. I decided we should maintain a platonic relationship. He never protested or discussed the subject. Well...I guess he simply agreed.

He said: "Don't believe in half of what you see or in half of what you hear." Then, he told me his story.

It was midnight when he joined the troops. Shadowy types crowded the meeting place. Some seemed rich, others poor, but all had that terminal look about them. The men knew they would challenge the natural forces that keep men on the ground. Major Chaos helped by pushing a few men out of the airplane. He hoped they made it back to the earth. He thought he saw one of them, an extremely light man, being drawn into space, but he couldn't be sure. When Major Chaos jumped, he held his guitar and played a slow song.

I remembered hearing a familiar tune coming from far

away the night before.

"You were better than many famous musicians," I said.

He finished his orange, ate the sandwich I prepared for him and had coffee. Later, he slept in front of the television, and I turned on the ceiling fan.

He has been here ever since. Nothing has changed between us, and I like it this way. Major Chaos is my piece of paradise. We clean the house and pay bills together. Sometimes we talk.

ONCE A MONTH WE PLAY

The donkey brays behind the guard's shack, once again challenging the myth about roosters being the first to tear the silence of dawn. We have constantly stumbled over truths we once so dearly adopted. The farm animals' roles keep changing according to their preferences. We were wrong, wrong, wrong to think that all donkeys or all roosters share the same nature.

Our objects, however, had mostly corresponded to our expectations. Only when our mothers came for a visit and released their sharp, straight-forward tongues, did we realize that the Russian Babushka dolls standing on our TV sets were no longer brilliant red, green, yellow and brown, but were merely reminding us of their origins through their fading paint, keeping the colors alive.

Sometime between the war's first and tenth year, we understood that nothing could surprise or disappoint us, as long as we did not change our perception of it. We revealed that newly-found truth to our mothers, who kissed us and suggested we take off the mirrors and hang pictures of our husbands in their place. When our mothers left, we replaced our husbands' pictures with images of our youth. This way, we knew, our innocence would remain eternal.

We are happy, happy, happy. Even while lying alone in a bubble bath, we go on referring to ourselves in the plural, as "we," and sometimes, "us." When we sing, our voices reach the skies.

We are free to raise our children, while our husbands protect the borders of our land. Husbands move from one battlefield to another, under pressure to keep in motion. We would accompany them, but children are moving inside us and out in their insecure ways. One may hang a line of dynamite over their necks, and they'll call it a collar. We give them bronze soldiers and take them out to play. My son—no, we cannot say he is ours—he takes a step, placing his round, funny legs too far apart from one another, and he balances and hangs on to us. We love him so much. So much.

We love our sons and husbands so much, we built walls around our land, so nobody would get hurt. One brick builds a guarantee for peace, a thousand mark our skyline.

We glue them with clay that sways like flesh and soon

turns solid. Our home seems strong to us, although we are not sure how firm it is. Husbands see the walls moving, closing on them, and they fire the guns, killing many husbands at a time.

Our strength lies in our unity. The certainty of having other survivors, husbands or otherwise, from the daily attack declines once we employ our knowledge of math. Instead, therefore, we focus on arts and entertainment. We celebrate the good life we have and the good years to come.

As years pass, we settle into odd numbers. Each of us young women has gone through the first year's mourning, the second year's recovery, an attempt at new relationships, and then nothing, or rather 'something' that we can't capture with words. We tried "loneliness," "void," and "vacuum" but the words broke in toothy shards and lost all that had been whole and vital about them.

We meet once a month, every month, always. If someone is missing, we know she has died. We ask the neighbors to keep an eye on our kids, and we plead with our mothers to keep company with our lonely mothers-in-law. They know how important it is; women cease to exist if they fail to attend a meeting.

We are trimmer than we used to be, our nails are manicured and our hair is dyed with quiet colors, as not to suggest we have forgotten. We kiss each other's cheeks and dig into our satchels for our young husbands' bronze soldiers, the ones they played with as kids. Our children have their own. We place the soldiers over the floor, trying a different strategy every month. We do not care which side wins, because we belong to both. Bang, bang bang. We laugh as we break each other's doll and then we break ours. We remove the headless, broken soldiers from the field, and place new ones in their place.

PEACE SIGNS

We raise wolf-like dogs and tiger-like cats and children who are not like us. We put peace signs around our yards, but nobody believes them. No, we are not warriors, but we're born to have no peace.

We go out barefoot, the sand burning like lit cigarette butts beneath our leathered feet. Our children fight through high school. Pacifists learn to shoot. We smoke and rage. And we eat to explosion. The children are beautiful and healthy. In them we will rebound.

We scuffle with neighbors on the right and on their right and on theirs. They put up peace signs too, and at night we meditate. The children have cucumbers, eggs and white cheese for dinner. We will pig out on more food when they are asleep. When they are awake, they watch over us. It is in them we trust.

Blazing fires on the western coast send us to our hoses, and peace signs, and children. It is time to try all three. On second thought, we hide the children until they grow up.

Then they will help us. In the meantime, we throw peace signs, and water, and we blanket little fires with our own hands.

The backyard is on fire. We occupy so much space, our wolves and tigers, and peace signs, and children are plunged to the front. We can save them from a future like ours. There is fire in our high bellies, in our heads and in our partners. We go for them. Sprinkled sunrays glow in another smoky afternoon.

CANNOT

And suddenly, it's fine to leave your husband, Rob, and your baby Dan, Dan from dandelion, Dan from Daniel and the lions, Dan from flowers and legends who have materialized into a baby enamored with your milk, whose screams wake you up like an alarm call, whose chirping of hatchlings are for anyone's smile. It's the 70s and we've had enough. You see, Rob's face is all country and farm, generations of hard workers from Europe of no edamame and soy but prey and hunger. And Europe, the other kind, is the place you'll go to follow the exact angles of Art Deco, and the colors, and mercurial fresh air spiraling in the lungs as you say, not "this is how I want to live" and discover you are pregnant, but "this is life" and it will be life without Rob, Rob from Robinson Crusoe, he says, Rob from Robbery, you say, and it is exactly that, a man, an island, a woman.

NATURE

When he woke up he chose a bedcover of a different color every day. I should have suspected his priorities, but I thought he was being an architect.

He moved me from place to place, to fit the space and the arrangement of the furniture. I curled on the couch until he sat me on an easy chair, splashed me atop the table, lay me on our bed, or asked me to act according to my senses and find my place.

I breathed his breath.

Once, I asked him why he chose me and not anyone beautiful, and he said that beauty existed in angles the way music burst out of silence.

It made me feel special. "I'm glad you don't need to change me," I said.

He laughed. His swimming-pool blue irises lit the fine wrinkles around his eyes, as if his laughter overflowed.

He told me stories. "You know," he said, "I was so used to the plains of Holland, that when I went skiing in the

Alps, I fainted, and when I did a trek in the Himalayas, I had a height sickness, and when I climbed the Andes, I became dizzy as if I'd been anesthetized.

His wiry arms made broad gestures, drawing the heights and depths of places outside.

"But you, you're a force of nature," he said and straightened my neck.

It was a free morning, so I felt the room and sat on a stool beside the TV set, my legs and arms angled in diamond shapes.

He nodded with satisfaction and covered the bed in silver. It was a cold day, and I shivered in my short-sleeved bride dress.

"Why do you want us to live in a penthouse?" I asked.

His laughter spilled over. Altitude was the most important thing in the world.

"It suits us!" he said, exhausting every possible answer.

He looked pale in the elevator, but was dashing in his suit. I had never seen such a wondrous golden cloud of hair like his.

"Are you well?" I asked since he seemed shaken.

"I've been to the roof of the world, so I can't complain

here."

"I think that the older we get, the more sensitive we become."

"When it's over, it's over. Worrying won't thicken the air."

One day, he'd evaporate like ether.

We continued with grace.

BOXING

They still had a lot of boxes from the move to their new place, so they had more boxes than friends.

"I'm all about boxes now. Enough with people," he said.

"For me, this is boxy enough," she said from her place under the country table.

"I can help you put the table back in a box," he suggested. It meant that he could see her. His voice wafted up from the right side of the living room, but she couldn't pinpoint his location.

"Well, we never were people's people, but why boxes?" she asked. She noticed a slight movement of a small one. He loved tightness. He usually tucked his blankets around him while she stretched her limbs out of hers.

An especially attractive box was standing outside on the terrace. It didn't escape him either.

"We can share the box," he said. "We're not too fat."

"Share?" she asked. The box was light blue, unlike all the brown ones. She always liked the solitude of a shoreline.

"Why? Do you fancy any box only for yourself?" he asked. She imagined him crinkling his nose like he had done a week earlier, in their old place, when she went to say goodbye to some friends as he left for work. He had also asked the same question.

"We'll see how it goes," she said. She took off her sneakers and threw them through the window, hoping nobody would witness the shoes landing in front of the lobby. People were too fussy and complicated and they could mess up your life.

RUNNING AWAY DIARY

Monday

I left a little late for work and hurried to the bus station, when I realized I couldn't remember where I worked. I looked at the route map and chose to go downtown. In one of the alleys, I met my son. He asked me what I was doing there. I told him I was at work. He said he was at school. We hooked our elbows together and went to an Arabic bar to have a Coke.

Tuesday

An old friend from high school, Rona Cohen, sent me an email full of memories I could not remember. I did not want to insult her, since she had been one of my best friends. I wrote her back, inventing more memories about people whose names she had mentioned. I wrote: "Do you remember how Arnon rang the bell of an old man's house like a madman? The old man chased after him screaming he'd kill every trespasser and they ran until I couldn't see them anymore."

She wrote back: "How could I forget? The old man died from a heart attack in the middle of the chase. It really marked me."

Wednesday

I carried a plastic bag full of sour cheese to the garbage can where I would not smell it. As I passed the gate, two boys chased a dog right at me. Its paws ripped the plastic bag, and the cheese covered us both. The boys ran away and the dog licked my shoes. I caressed its back until it finished eating.

Thursday

My daughter said we were out of water. I showed her the mineral water standing beside the yellow mustard.

She peeked at it and said, "We're out of everything."

Friday

A baby-girl with soft cheeks raised her large eyes to me. Her mother was smoking and drinking coffee by a café's counter. I picked up the baby and held her to my chest. She rested there with trust for a moment, then started screaming.

The smoking woman snatched her away. "What is it with you?" she asked.

I said, "I'm sorry. I could not help it."

Friday

When I looked up, the family was gone. I turned on the TV and watched a woman having a breakdown in an open field. I turned off the TV. Instead, I read a short story by an American writer, whose name was lost on me. It was about adultery. I took the daily paper. The weather prediction was that of too much rain.

Friday

The telephone rang. Before I said anything, a man said, "Sorry. It's a wrong number."

Thursday

A man with a brown stash of hair started following me. He went everywhere I did, keeping a few steps behind me, and when I was home, he waited behind the thick bushes and peeped into the house. I didn't mind it. I opened the window to invite him in for dinner. But when I looked out, the bushes were gone, and the street stretched long and empty.

Friday

I kissed the postman. I kissed the man who delivers the gas cylinders. I kissed the Sedex man. I kissed the neighbor who e to collect money. I kissed the mirror. All the lips were cold.

Saturday

I bought myself a birthday card with a little joke about going over the hill to pick flowers. I signed the card and went to the post office to send it. I never received it.

Sunday

I passed by a glass door and saw myself, with a prettier face, playing ping-pong inside. I wanted to go in and play, but knew I would lose, so I left.

Friday

I finally got mail. It was a rejection of my application for a Philosophy course at the local university. I had not applied anytime I could remember, but suddenly it seemed like a good idea. I looked the university up in the telephone book and Golden Pages, and then at Google.

Such university did not exist.

Thursday

Nothing happened. I mean: nothing. Not the slightest wind, a barking dog, a passing man, nothing. The clock was stuck on 7:25. If I died then, nobody would have noticed.

Sunday

I was resting in bed when I heard steps in the empty house,

crossing the room from the left to the right, the way it would sound through a sound system at a good cinema. The steps grew quick and urgent. I opened my eyes. The sound did not come from anyone walking, but from my own feet.

CRYSTAL AND GOLD

The mutts' coarse barks break the furious sound of waves, crushed against each other by intersecting winds. The storm shrieks among rocks and bushes but it must die at the end of the night. In the morning, I'll fling the window open to find the sun resting atop a pine tree, indifferent to the stinging green needles.

My hope runs loose like a damp street dog.

My youngest daughter's slender arm is curled over my belly. My oldest is propped up on her elbows, staring at the shadow's dance above. Chrissie is my youngest; the oldest girl is Gill. I may be reciting their original names, or maybe the storm has melded their names and given them new homes. I am not that lucid anymore.

In past times, each day stretched like our hammocks, and he and I interlaced and formed a carpet for our daughters. They bloomed, they grew on power, they needed more than we could give. Their command made us a carpet blown by Jinn into air.

They befriended passersby whose names they could hardly remember. Their clothing bore names of prosperous strangers. They almost fell down the holes torn in the lace of each day. We were about to lose them by the time the storm began.

The truck arrived to take us to a shelter, to protect us from a devastating rain (though not from whipping gazes of officials).

"We stay at our home," I said. The squeaking of the metal gate made my Crystal shiver. My man, their father, said: "Off we go."

I motioned: No.

"This is home," echoed my Gold. I thought: there's hope.

He said, "Let's leave. They are a piece of my flesh, and you and I are one as well."

"They are not a piece of anyone. Nor am I."

His glinting teeth split a bitter smile. "Please!" he implored. "They shouldn't struggle and suffer. They'll break."

"They are women. Their defeat takes more than rain."

"They don't need your drama. There will be swamps,

sickness and cold."

"No."

Crystal shook against my shoulder. Gold rested her head in the slope of my neck. I held them like babies. Their warm faces, sweaty and trusting, sank against my waist.

His tea-brown eyes, so much like theirs, caressed us three. "I don't understand," he said. "But fine, I'll come for you in a few days."

"Yes, go. When the water is down, come back."

Ever since, the water has risen so high, our house has become a mushroom in a swampy land. Tonight, the flood must stop, and the siege should break. We occupy the humid second story above the flooded first floor. The scent of cold and of water is slippery, more perceived than smelled. For thirty days, our walls have kept us safe. They should let us out in due time, the way my body once released my girls.

I keep dreaming his sorrow and his smile, his enveloping arms. I wonder if he could reach us if he tried.

Under the woolen blanket, I cross my leg with Crystal's and put my arm over Gold. My husband will find us knitted together like a braid.

There is little potable water and less food. Every dawn

we look for the first sunray as if it were a sign, and every day we find it and smile. Like freedom seekers, we are against the madness of higher powers.

I burn with fever.

Crystal turns her lovely face to me. "Are you thirsty?" she asks.

"The first thing I'll do when the water is down is make us soup." Gold laughs.

They decide to transport me to town. They will build a raft with the broken trunks that hit the walls outside.

I say, "We may be imprisoned, but we are still alive."

Gold's eyes seek the light. "The window frames an image of still life," she says. Her eyelashes close like sickles.

Crystal takes my hand in hers. Her touch is softer than mine. It is time for him to come for us.

I am waiting for the morning. For his breath of relief.

ZIP

His fingers run over the trumpet as if he's not one to have
cereal in the morning, or someone like her, no. His jeans
are slashed above the knees and his shirt sticks to muscles
in motion. He used to be a tanker, but now he lies in bed
with fleas and women, sometimes with icicles to ease his
hangovers. He sings a melancholic Russian song in its
Hebrew translation and brings back the Jerusalem fortune
teller who tells her she'd lose lovers, one of them young,
others younger. But they didn't die on her, nor will they.
Now she knows it. As his fingers unzip her, the lovers fall
out one by one.

THE LAST TIME

She puts on the new dress before going to him, before paying
another debt. It is not personal nor can it be measured.
Taffeta in royal green clings to her breasts and crashes toward
her olive high-heeled sandals in a high wave. By looking
at her, nobody would guess. She'll get so naked, she'll be
untouchable.

THE STRING THEORY

Last month, our favorite airline (CMN: usually cheap, rarely retires airplanes) started employing rag dolls instead of air hostesses. My husband and I were reluctant to fly with them again, since we dislike alterations and surprises, masqueraded gates to disappointments. But we had to visit his aging parents, and changing companies would have defied our steadiness and our sense of loyalty as well. Habit triumphed.

My husband frowned at the grey rag doll tagged Sharon that let us onto the airplane. She was standing on a high stool to reach a regular human height. I couldn't find any apparent division between her body and clothes, but the waist was full enough to convey her femininity, and her lower stomach had the shape of a skirt.

"Don't let it bother you. We'll make the best of this flight," I whispered to my husband to help him go through the worry phase he tends to explore deeper every passing year.

"I guess they'll do," my husband replied in a low voice as he handed his umbrella to a beige rag doll. "The regular air hostesses are only nice to the passengers of the first class anyway."

"See?"

"They aren't even as attractive as they used to be."

"Fine." I straightened my new dress and arranged my hair, then sat down near the window and he sat by the aisle. The rag dolls attended us, cleverly disguising the fact they couldn't speak. They floated with the help of transparent springs so they could serve drinks and food when someone or something blocked the aisle.

My husband received the extra pillows and blankets he requested, as well as more tea, and he had the rag dolls turn on his light and insert his headphones. Nobody had ever pampered him that much. It seemed as if a flock of rag dolls were serving him, but perhaps only one poor doll came and left a hundred times. He looked happy.

A blue rag doll with a name tag saying "Sharon III" floated and threw confetti as if we were there to party. Looking up, we came to understand that she was simply falling apart, shedding crumpled pieces of cloth. It brought back an image I'd rather have forgotten of our drunken friends at the New Year's Eve party. Of course, they put their rags back on when they came out of our swimming pool.

"All the key people should learn how efficient and attentive are these dolls," said my husband, his eyes like bonfires. "I have to pull some strings."

I passed my fingers down his spine to the hook. "Leave it to me," I said.

GET DOWN TO IT

The Italian pasta and the ginger seem safe, but the flour and the beans have already been infested with tiny balls that crush between your fingers like dwarf-cockroaches.

At first, they appeared in the children's artworks. We had hoped to show the art in the future to let the world see that our pride wasn't vanity but recognition of geniuses in creation. Instead, the dwarves took over.

We squeezed them and threw bloody bits of art away, speculating that they liked the glue, made of flour and water and all the peas and noodles the children used as material. But then, they advanced to the books. They devoured Mark Twain, Doris Lessing, Ben Hecht, and Thomas Mann. While eclectic, they never touched thrillers and ghost stories. They also avoided our ancient and new Bible editions.

When our shelves were half-empty and the children's desks all cleaned-up, the dwarves moved to the closet for a short visit we never solved. They appeared here and there, as if calling for our fists to come down on them, which we did with the righteousness of a stoned surfer catching his nightmare policeman smoking dope. But the dwarf survivors didn't spread the rumor to their friends or family. The whole tribe and some visitors made an inexplicably unseen journey from the second floor to the first and settled down in the kitchen.

According to The All Bug-Theory they should have gone for the whole wheat products first, but again, they surprised us and populated the tea bags. Then, they went for the biscuits, and now, their direction is clear. We almost sympathize with the poor bastards. What a hurdle it is to pretend you like artworks and books when all you really want is to get down to the garbage.

SOAP

Little bursts of laughter explode between the twin couches
and around the table. I didn't clean after last night's visit.
Crumbs of salt crackers and laughter still roll over my floor.

The laughing sound does not belong here.

Long ago I left home while the family was watching TV.
They didn't even notice. I closed the door on the fake TV
laughter. When I called a week later, my mother asked if I'd
be back in time for *Soap*.

I imagined my father and my mother falling in love and
then buying a TV set to pass the years.

Ever since, I have stood on the beach every morning and
looked at the passing clouds carrying light from my sea to
cities that have no ocean. My ears have held the sound of the
waves the way seashells do.

People used to tire me.

I was wary of the family visit as I arranged the plates, the
silverware, the wine and the water glasses not for myself, as

usual, but for fifteen people.

My family seemed oversized, because the news about each newborn had skipped me. News floats like clouds, and if you sleep you miss it.

We made a toast to happiness. When the cheers dissolved into idle noise, I asked my family to be quiet for a moment and listen. We heard the permanent humming that rises beyond the silence.

"What a buzz," my cousin said.

"People say it's the voice of the universe," said my sister.

"Do people talk about it?" I wondered. I thought they were busy watching TV.

"Please fill my glass," my mother asked. She smiled. "How would you know about conversations?"

My father touched my arm.

My sister's baby cried and she got up. Babbling and mumbling erupted from the corner where she changed his diapers. My brother talked about a new TV series and teased his wife. She told me, "You really should buy yourself a television."

Before I replied, my uncle said he'd brought his. They sat on the twin couches and joined their laughter with the TV's canned one. I imagined they saw me on the screen.

"Go back to the table," I said from the TV's belly.

"Stay with me," a stunning blond man told me. I realized he was my lover for the series.

He kissed me hard. The family held their breaths.

I slapped him, because I was surprised.

The laughter burst from all sides. I did not stay with him long enough to see what followed.

My niece chased after my cousin.

"Pass the salt," my father asked. He hummed an old song from a movie.

I felt their cheer, refreshing like the salty spray of a broken wave.

Today I take a bath, and bits of laughter burst out of the water. I try to touch them, but they slip between my fingers.

OUT OF ORDER

I dial Information to ask for my in-laws' phone number. I used to call their place when my husband and I were first dating, but once he moved in with me I forgot their number. It's Freudian, you might say. So?

I had just inherited my parents' place. The flat was full of old furniture, carpets, photo albums, and clothes. Wine, vodka, and brandy bottles stood in the cupboard at attention.

I was at a loss. I couldn't give away anything, because that stuff was all I had left of my parents. I couldn't sell the objects, either, because then they'd belong to strangers. I'd rather birch myself.

At the same time, I sensed a conflict of interests. My own place was a temple to minimalism, every last bit measured, dyed, and calculated to fit in with everything else. You might say it's a reaction to my childhood's house, the little porcelain dolls and small straw animals filling every space, and that it's completely Freudian. Maybe so.

I had been sitting on the living room Persian carpet, a weaving of kelp-like forms, looking through air, when I saw it: light at the end of the tunnel. You see, not every cliché goes wrong.

In the momentary trance I had reached an epiphany. I realized that by joining my parents' stuff with my in-laws' I'd honor the parental generation, add to the family union, and keep the precise order at my place. One day, my husband and I would deal with it all.

So now I stood in the dining room, right by the kitchen, dialing the information service. Three rings later a very young voice answered. I gave him my in-laws' names and address and asked for their number. (The Internet was irrelevant, inexistent yet.)

"I don't think I should give it to you," the voice said.

"What?"

"Hahaha...Fine. It's 223-9878."

I stared at the telephone. "I don't think this is the right number. Their area's numbers start with 335," I said.

"Busted!" he screamed. "Haha!"

I drew my ear away from the yelling receiver.

"So, what do you say, you and me, closed curtains, a

38

bottle of wine?" he asked.

"Is this Information?" I had dialed correctly, surely, but the young voice didn't seem to belong there.

"Yes it is! Yes it is!"

I kicked the refrigerator's door open. An old onion spread its grown leaves around the bulb like a squid. This brought some reminiscences from the past.

"I need my in-laws' phone number," I said.

"Ask your husband!" he howled.

"He thinks I should deal with it on my own."

"So let's get together, you and me," he cried with exaggerated excitement.

"I...." What else can you say?

"Do you flirt like this all the time?" he demanded.

"How old are you?" The telephone company seemed shakier than ever.

"I'm thirteen," he yelled.

"How on earth did you get on my line?"

"Your own telephone service! Hunky telephone!"

I kicked the refrigerator door closed and the dining room turned darker. I missed cheese omelets and avocado sandwiches. The chocolate cake had a European scent.

"We demand control over the city!" the boy screamed.

"I could probably be your mother," I said.

"And I could be your Oedipus," he shouted.

I took a deep breath. "Listen, dear. It's an emergency. I need to join my inheritance with my husband's. What's the telephone number?"

He was silent for once. Then he hung up on me.

Everything had gone out of order. Prodigious hackers had taken over the city. They could get hold of everything we owned, by confusing documents, files, and telephone numbers. Perhaps nobody was due inheritance any more. My parents had left too much, anyway, more than I could take, more than I needed.

I imagined the telephone service kid, red-headed perhaps, looking right through the door's peephole with a periscope.

He'd watch me grab a photo album with photographs from the times you could get in touch with your parents by crying out. All you had to do was as simple as drinking squeezed grapefruit juice while sitting with them on a sunlit balcony.

HEAR ME

My cousin, they say (benevolent people from a shadowy side), has left me a letter before he died.

I am thrilled beyond words, as I grab the envelope with greedy fingers. He did think about me! He did love me! He did leave me something to live on, a remembrance of our years in the fields and gardens of his little town, my winters in the old pajamas he passed on, his endless tease and discreet care. The distance of seven years stretched between us, and the closeness of siblings, and something special, like an all-night conversation between two strangers.

I unglue the envelope, look in, and let the contents roll out.

How can a flat envelope contain a grilled chicken?

The juicy golden thighs stick to the paper. Well-browned wings roll aside. The chest lies on the stomach. There's even a head adorned by a nice beak, but otherwise ordinary, only grilled, which is unusual. Of course, I don't even notice the facial details at first. This whole thing doesn't make me think about chickens.

I'm deciphering the message. He was an amateur chef; this is my clue. Still, it's hard to believe that chefs conceal messages in chickens. Or that a chicken is a message.

Then again, why is this chicken so unlike others? What is he trying to tell me, but can't because I don't get it?

A chicken isn't worth a thousand words or any words at all, and I can only read.

So I'm asking. When will I receive one of his rare calls, so madcap and endearing, and how will I reconcile the ceaseless mocking and the bursting warmth? Where is the life that broke and disappeared, still special?

I look once more to confirm the envelope isn't empty.

SOMEWHERE STATION

After everything that had passed between us, I was only too glad to watch the clouds under me. These soft grey ships with an orange edge were beautiful.

I had to bring home at least one baby. I failed to have one of my own.

The woman next to me was very fat as if she had eaten all the ice cream I had avoided for years. I never wanted to get chubby. Her plump body undulated, liquid-like, to all sides. I felt her belly next to my elbow, and imagined it as very white under the tent- size dress she was wearing.

On her other side, a very mousy little man watched the movie attentively. His eyes bulged out each time Uma Thurman appeared on the screen. If he had danced with her, his head would have been leaning comfortably against her belly button.

The woman turned her round face to me and with a very delicate voice asked if I wanted a gum. She said it eased the ear pressure. I refused politely and again took a deep dive into the clouds, feeling the last warmth of daylight.

Not long afterwards, she turned to me once more and offered me chocolate. Now I found her so nice and friendly that I was willing to share the whole package with her. The mousy man she called Max was absorbed with the film.

The chocolate tasted great, as sweet as the smiling woman. She broke it, and we ate thoughtfully every melting piece.

"Good, huh?" she asked me again and again, and I, mouth full, nodded approvingly.

Feeling much sweeter by the middle of the chocolate bar, I chatted with her. Her words came out in a unique order, captivating my attention. In her mellow way, she described their pastoral home by the blue mountains. A house full of shouting kids. First sons and daughters, then grandsons and granddaughters.

In the mornings they all played in the dense forest behind the house. They were a part of the wildlife of the wood. She would stay home, cooking and baking, mixing and tasting all kinds of wonderful flavors.

"And you," she asked pleasantly, "wouldn't you like to have kids around?"

My old sadness returned, and as she looked at me, I found myself crying. She held my shoulders, humming and comforting me as if I were one of their children.

Once her warmth melted that hardened spot in my belly, I fell asleep in peace. I woke up to a special sound, and looked around me. The couple was not there. The voices came from the front, the unmistakable sounds of passionate lovemaking. The woman called out intimate nicknames, saying he was soooo good. She moaned, shamelessly, and made a happy pigeon's cooing. The man urged her to come, to take him, gladly making his own love-sounds. They had fun, more fun than I thought possible.

Laughter spilled involuntarily out of my throat. I recognized the woman's voice. Yes, and the film was over.

The other passengers were sleeping now. Here and there, a light shined, but the place was calm and quiet. I sat there, laughing to myself, imagining the two having adventurous sex on the plane.

Excited screams burst from the front, as they had a powerful climax almost at the same time. I wondered if they would be embarrassed upon their return to the seats.

When they did show up, the woman smiled at all

directions, and the man had a self-contented, satisfied smile on his face.

"Here you are," said the woman. She brought out a bundle, a moving blanket from somewhere in her tent-dress. I took it. By god!!! It was a baby, looking at me with huge eyes. And smiling.

"And one more," she said. This one was sleeping, his curly hair resting humidly on his newborn's lovely forehead. I was so moved, I started crying again.

"They are for you," the little man reassured me.

The couple looked at me and at each other with their calm, warm eyes.

"Would you like some more?" she asked me.

"We can make them easily," he said, smiling at her in a playful sort of way.

"Oh!" I was sobbing. "Only one more. It will be wonderful!"

By the end of the flight I had three little babies, sleeping deeply. They were healthy and beautiful. My breasts seemed to blossom in the sunrise warmth, and filled with it.

My mission was complete, for me, for my man, and for any cravings I'd had.

The couple still calls sometimes. They ask me if I want any more kids. I always laugh, and tell them they don't have to use this old excuse again.

THE SPIRIT OF HIS WILL

I was born inside Jim Morrison, languidly parting from the inner walls of the belly he grew in his last years. Birth pain wracked him when my spirit broke through his. He fell to his knees, hitting the earth, and his contracting muscles brought me to my first climax.

Already a woman, I rested between his soft tissues and drifted safely in my blood-nurtured temple. Within the delicate lace of our veins, I could not differentiate his thoughts from mine, his fingerprints from my bodylines. Witchcrafted, my flesh was transformed by his verses to mirror his desire. I trailed into his dreams, unwrapping fine veils of flesh to tie his lyrics with my umbilical cord. Soon his voice penetrated my thinning skin, burning and aging both mine and his.

I breathed: "Pain is the one thing that overpowers time. Can we have more?"

"We can."

The echo of the crowds' cries thrashed his walls, moving

back and forth like a maddened ball without a hitter. Deadly tongues of strangers flickered at us from street corners and journal stands.

Turning heavy, we sank into non-existent swamps. Down by the bottom, we peeled life of its every layer of magic. We spun in the center of the bubbling grounds to embrace the death that tiptoed behind us. Oh, sweet intoxication!

Yet even in the heat of our death-lust, we meticulously considered stage, scenery and lighting for the final act. No others could transcend time; only the two of us.

He gave the finger to potential saviors.

When the sky turned orange and betrayed a growing heat, his oxygen swirled in my lungs leaving him breathless. I whispered my promise of eternity into the air that suffocated him. No other Ophelia had ever outlived her lover, drawing the breath of his agony.

In Paris, the city of romance and decay, of poetry and drains, we joined earth to earth, ash to ash by way of honoring the Greek history of orgies. Consuming our love in the wilderness of after-death, we called poets and lovers to split the ground and dive in with us.

While time dissolved into liquid, his heart poured juices

into mine. Soon from the richness of his body—opened from chest to crotch, sweet as a ripe passion fruit—I grew and bloomed underneath the cemetery, spreading as grass throughout the cities of his dreams. My arms reached for his love but it no longer had physical boundaries. Sprouting from his every vein, my long tendrils sprang sending delicate strings to wrap around the men and women that once were his public. In the unity of their cries, my lover materialized.

WINGS

Remembrance.

Swarms of locusts spread over our parents' lands like the wings of a huge bird. First, they invaded the wheat's reign, then, moved to the cornfields.

As soon as we saw the black insects, we recognized them as our demons. Their passage left our heads light and open for pure air. New clarity chased our shadows away. We relaxed, more than we imagined possible.

On their journey, the demons devoured every plant.

They lived the moment fully, the way we always desired. It felt good. It verged on perfection. We watched them with paternal pride.

They were ugly, as demons mostly are, but they did not know it. Nor did we. We couldn't define their existence as ugliness at the time. We danced around the fields holding spoons and pans in our hands, hitting the metal in a rhythmic play. It did not shake them.

Drained of demons, our hollow bodies sucked in so

much air, we started floating. Reaching a safe altitude, we formed an out-caste circle.

(Storytellers would say we saw the town from a different point of view.)

We raised our faces toward the mellow sun. Could it burn our wings? We looked down.

Our parents set the fields on fire. Hell broke free. The locusts didn't leave, but moved to other areas. Some of them burned like living torches, others, like sacrificed witches in the old times. Their crackling bodies sounded like Spanish castanietas.

Most of them wandered to new shelters. Deserting us, they left us shaken.

The fire swallowed the oxygen that kept us up, and we landed on the ground one by one. Demonless, we felt lonely. When we ran to our parents, thirsty for hugs, they did not recognize us.

SUDDEN CHANGES

Nothing has changed since the bird migration twenty years ago. The ocean has been generous to us, as have the fields, the women, and the rains. We work hard and sleep heavily. Our bodies develop a brute strength. Strict and moral but always kind, some of us, men, have commanded the town.

One day, the rain stops and no train arrives. The transition finds us solid, healthy, caring for big families and large households. The winds bring a smell of stinking fish from the east and howls of hungry hyenas from the west. Our present threatens to overpower our experience and catch a future we can't even guess.

Women look in vain for fish to smoke and preserve in salt. The fruit in our orchards bursts open in the heat, shedding sweet meat to the ground. We wait at the train station, ready to serve the tourists we once abhorred. The railway stretches empty toward a far city where passengers are kept away by rumors of disease.

Over the second full moon, the footsteps of external

force cross our path. We consider ways to survive, but threat cuts the air like a slicing knife. Women overwhelm us when they react to the urge of time. Their bodies blossom and open like sea anemones, moving round and mature limbs. Their fruity scent maddens us to the point we lose words like loyalty or betrayal. Our erections rise under our loosened clothes; we want our neighbors' wives.

Their spread legs expose mango-like vaginas gleaming with juice. Craving to drink, we approach with tongues stuck-out to lick and suck and gulp it in. Their fluids slip inside our hot bodies like nectar. Wrapped in their legs and arms, our drugged bodies lull in their softness until a burst of semen wakes us from a dreamless sleep.

On the dusty streets and in sandy backyards the desert closes upon us. Food is scarce but women's juices maintain us. They feed the children with hyena's meat and rotten fruit. We watch them devouring the leftovers. Their appetite for us weakens as their bellies fill with new life. We are on the verge of despair. We cry for them, but they listen to different voices. They step over us, heavy with their loads.

Lusting, we roll on the streets, thirsty for our women. The wind strokes our abrasive bodies with delicate layers of salty sea-sand. The cries of newborns beat our thinning voices. Our women breastfeed the babies and each other. And we are aroused. Their bodies, having lost the avocado shape of pregnancy, move with endless grace. Their skin is silken and their hair is smooth.

We have lost the command of nature's signs, are grateful when each woman takes her man home.

They send the children out and look at their men with glimmering eyes. Before entangling their bodies with ours, they intoxicate us with an earthy scent. Thrusting our heads between their thighs, eager like babies we suckle. Raising our eyes, we watch them watching us with maternal smiles.

Two:

MINUTE LIFE LENGTH

THE FUTURE OF COLOR

Many nights I dread his future color, my alertness

pronouncing itself in prayers to a doubtfully existent God.

These nights of a not-yet-mother trespass daytime.

At work, I pull back from the mud-colored poverty, not

wanting the stories of lost battles. I say I will do my best but

I know my best is never effective. I am a social worker who is

losing faith in change.

Back at home, the slums crawl into my dreams. I cry and

turn to all the religions for support.

Days pass, counted according to the medical calendar:

seven, 15, 45.

Under an exquisitely hot sun, I make the two-mile walk

to the doctor's office.

"What are the chances?" I ask him.

He has coffee-colored skin, already wrinkled in places,

big glasses and an air of pride.

"I don't understand your concern," he says.

"You don't?"

He stays silent.

Soon the time comes to see my son. Once I am lying in front of the ultrasound screen, I close my eyes.

"Tell me he has my color, the color of Ken, the doll," I want to say. "The color that is unquestionably accepted." I mean to say it but I don't. "What does he look like?" I finally ask. My fingers squeeze my eyeballs until I see red and yellow dots.

"He looks perfectly healthy," the doctor says. "He has everything he needs at this stage, and everything is in place. You can open your eyes now."

I look at the black-and-white screen and see my baby son in a fetal position.

"Oh!" I say.

"I love him," I don't say. The words slide back inside.

***

I speak to my baby when I feel him pressing against my insides. "Your father and I became one, the way darkness and light absorb each other in the exchange of day to night. That 'one' is you, our baby."

There was a father with a deep color, unlike my pale one. He had chocolate tones of skin and palpable warmth that lingered underneath.

Yes, there was a father, but there isn't any longer.

I dread the day my skin the color of sea sand will not clothe my son. Even so, he will never be one of the kids who linger under the city bridge or in the strategically located crossroads. He will not have to use his infantile charm to receive food. No. He will be the one dot of color in the classroom of a private school.

Day No. 200 brings a chilling wind. From the bus, going to work, I see children getting out of cars in front of the school's entrance. I want to celebrate: I'm purchasing my first car today. I can't celebrate. My mind goes back to the talk-show celebrity interviewing a cocoa-colored millionaire.

When he drives his Mercedes, the millionaire says, people think he works as a driver. He told the truth, I could tell. The interviewer and the audience laughed. He laughed too. He started as an office boy and worked his way up to a place where he can laugh.

I am driving my new car when my son starts moving. It is the only discomfort I have ever loved. My body is our home. "You see, baby, inside we are the same. You shoot my belly up toward my heart, and all my body twists although I am not moving."

I dread the time he will find out colors have meanings. He must not notice our different skins. They will be there, for the world to pass judgment on, but not for us.

"Together we embody my past and your future. You will be safe with me."

I must be strong.

I tell him about his father. "He wasn't handsome, but his eyes and mouth, his hair and waist and limbs and skin had the truest look, a strong sense of living. I knew his touch before he touched me, and when we loved, it was love. If you ever ask, I'll tell you more, but you may choose not to ask. What's the point in knowing anything else but that you are the fruit of this kind of love?"

***

I still count the days according to the medical calendar and according to my own as well. I feel our mutual motion at nights, when the womb's undulation lulls us both to better dreams. We grow, my son and I grow up.

It is the night of the 290th day, and it is a good night.

I cannot be afraid any longer.

When it gets dark, I let my body rest against the pillows

on my bed. The night lamp sheds tender light, and the posters of Kandinsky and Miró color my white walls with festive colors.

My son. Never fear.

THE WAY THINGS ARE

When her mother first shut up, Dana took a deep breath of relief. Silence was better than shouts, a matter of priorities, like choosing classical music over the news.

Her father was pale. His chest heaved as it had done in the intervals between her mother's shouts, then sunk like an emptied balloon.

Their silence started low, like a mellow Italian baritone, but by Friday it cut through like a soprano-sharp blade.

Dana kept hoping that now that they stopped fighting over bills her dad couldn't pay or had neglected, he'd admire her mother's beauty again and say that she shamed flowers with her grace. But even she realized that Adel's face wasn't smooth now and didn't look in full blossom. Her lips remained narrow and tight and she had an angry line between her eyebrows. Isaac must have noticed it too.

On Friday, he gave Dana a little kiss on her cheek. He was going to say something, but instead, he left.

Dana heard the truck start. She opened the door and

called out after him: "Wait! I want a ride."

"Another day," he said and drove away.

Adel ran out and called him mad and irresponsible and.... Her gaze landed on Dana, and she swallowed deadly words.

Once, a bee had stung Dana and dropped dead onto the ground (then Dana smashed it with her red sandal). What if people like us used up their hearts?

But Mom took her in and made her lemonade. Dana got busy with a doll and a rope and a plastic bus. Only later did she realize Adel had left and was taking too long to come back.

Dana stumbled on an armchair, as she rushed out and stopped dead in the garden. Adel was squatting on the ground, holding so many milkweeds, they were falling out of her arms, and still, she went on plucking and picking up flowers one after the other, pulling out the whole plant with its roots. The long stems scratched her cleavage.

"Mom, what are you doing? Mom?"

Adel glanced at Dana, and Dana looked from her reddened eyes to the ground. Where the flowerbeds had bloomed, the soil was turned over and worms were seeking shelter.

Adel smiled at her. "We'll put them in vases so they'll stay beautiful," she said.

Isaac would have told her to leave the flowers alone. "Mom, they'll whither. They'll die, Mom. Let's plant them back."

Adel placed the flowers between them, a hill of them, a mountain, and said, "We'll be fine."

Dana caressed the petals of a flower. "Dad will come back quickly," she said, arranging the leaves. She studied the flower and added, "It's beautiful."

Then she took one step backwards because Adel was looking at her as if she had run into an old friend inside Dana. She was glowing with the same expression of surprise and pleasure she had that other day when she met Henry from England.

Dana pushed the flower into the mound.

Adel held out her hand for Dana's hand, or for the flower. She said, "That's just the way things are."

PERFECT FOR THIS WORLD

My mother watched *Gone With the Wind* about 15 times, but she only paid for her first viewing.

Like me, all the kids used to go to the movies every Tuesday, accompanied by their mothers.

In Israel, in the 60s, there was a recess in the middle of each film. The kids usually stood in line to buy popcorn while the mothers went together to the ladies' room.

However, to my discreet sorrow, my mother acted differently.

On our first trip to *Gone With the Wind* she went into the film projector room during the recess, and returned only after the lights went back off.

She was a beautiful woman, and we never had to pay for a movie ticket again. (And mind you, I watched the same movie three more times before I finally stopped accompanying her.)

***

My mother learned important lessons from the film. She

took down the living room curtains and sewed them into a pretty dress for herself and a nice suit for me. She mastered the sewing machine perfectly.

Evidently, Scarlett O'Hara had great success with her velvet curtain dress. My case was different. The building where we lived consisted of small apartments arranged around an open patio, and the patio kids always stayed in each other's homes. That's how everyone knew that my suit had been made of curtains.

"Now that you have a suit, will your mom use your clothes as curtains?" Jacob asked.

Nastier suggestions followed. Joe, the oldest boy, asked if my mom's bra could cover the bare living room window.

Three times I arrived home marked with signs of fighting. I claimed it had been a fight over a boy, because I knew my mother would admire that. She was a romantic, after all. I experienced hard times, but she seemed so proud of our new clothes, and I had no heart to refuse her gift. How could I? She said I was the most wonderful princess she had ever dressed.

And business had never been better. My mother had developed a delicate marketing strategy, after she realized how impressed the neighbors were by her ability to create clothes. Soon, many living rooms lost their curtains, to be replaced with straw blinds, and the women brought the fabric to Mom. She invited "the ladies" (as she called them) for tea and involved them in light conversation.

My mother was the only daughter of a professor of literature, as well as a dancer, and she had inherited the brilliance of both. As a result, she easily charmed anyone around her. When the women felt completely at ease, she told them the price of the clothes. At that point, nobody could have refused her anything.

To please my mother, the only thing I had to do was be good at whatever I did. When I decided, at the age of six, that I wanted to join a circus, my mom made me train every day. I put mattresses on the patio, jumped, rolled, stood on my hands and on my head and tried to attract an audience. I escaped mockery because some of the other kids decided to join me. While Mom conducted the small business affairs that rendered us a minimum amount of comfort, I dedicated myself to my future profession.

After a month or so, we, the circus players, felt confident enough to put on a show. One sunny afternoon, our mothers and two or three unemployed fathers bought tickets for the big event. We said that the money would be used for charity. As most of our families lived off small pensions of all sorts, it was true enough. The show started at exactly 4 p.m. We made a pyramid, performed spicy clown jokes, walked on our hands in a zigzag formation and manipulated marionettes. We performed with great skill and received yells and applause from our astonished crowd. When I looked up, I saw my mother smiling and clapping her delicate hands, as charming as ever.

After everyone had gone home for dinner, my mother sat at the wooden table and asked me to join her. I suspected that she had something serious to tell me.

"Darling," she said, "was the circus your idea?"

"You know it was, Mom."

"Hadn't you started training long before the others joined you?"

"Not really," I said. "Maybe a week earlier."

"A week is a long time," she said. "Don't you agree that you're the best athlete and the funniest clown?"

Of course I didn't object. Instead, I agreed enthusiastically.

"So why," she finished dramatically, "why were you not the star? Why did I have to look for you among the others?"

She caught me by surprise. I hadn't given it a single thought. I had enjoyed performing in the circus so much, I hadn't wished it differently.

"Well?" she asked.

"It was fun, Mom," I said.

"Fun!" she mimicked me. "Fun! How will you survive in this world?"

The words were familiar, and they didn't have the impact my mom had probably meant them to have. I knew she would always be there for me. She was so beautiful, so smart and strong. She would protect me, a plump little girl with problems in math.

Sometimes I asked my mother from whom I inherited my looks, my difficulties in school, my awkwardness. And she would answer: "Your father, too, had to struggle his way around, darling. May angels guard his soul."

I understood that my dad had already gone to heaven because he had not been suited for this world.

Now I edit cookbooks. I never use curtains as background in my photographs. They remind me of *Gone*

With the Wind.

I sometimes recall how my mom showed me the ways to win in this world. I remember that she said I shouldn't express emotion. It is very likely that she was right.

During the years that followed the big circus show, I tried to follow the paths of my mother's practical mind. I was not surprised when I grew taller and received good grades at school. I knew that I could go further than anyone else. Because I was fortunate enough to be her daughter, everything was possible.

That was why I was so shocked when my mother became sick. She refused to go to the hospital because, she said, she knew better than the doctors what was best. My French aunt hired a nurse to help her. My mother was not pleased. It was more than we needed, as she put it.

It took my mother three months to die. For three months she repeated everything she had ever taught me and added some new ideas. She looked like a skeleton at that stage, and I was afraid. Nevertheless, she held on—alive and talkative—until she felt that I might survive without her.

Then she kissed my tears, said she trusted me to win and died. It was all done according to her precisely calculated timing.

She was perfect for this world.

TINY LOVE STORIES

I.

The boy's little bump under the jeans is distracting and disgusting, a forbidden adventure, a gummy danger.

Her mind drifts in the guessing of a possible perfect harmony. They will talk and laugh, and he'll see only her in a room full of children.

She penetrates his halo, dancing with him. A silken night promises more. He reclines on a sofa. The bump under his pants is round like the Russian neighbor's back as he gorges on a drink.

The girl's first love story will be abstract.

II.

The king of the class tells her he knows that she'll love him. He is so confident, she suspects it may be true.

She rolls over a five-step wooden horse at the gym to keep his eyes on her. But he has eyes for everyone.

He sings, standing on coral like a rooster. She is his hen.

She never tells him.

He ends up with a daughter of hippies, a girl known at school as a nymphomaniac.

The girl will pass many years, distracted and disgusted by their probable wild sex.

III.

When the boys (the police) catch the girls (the thieves), they pull at the straps of their bras. Only she hides behind a mound of thick bushes so they won't find the thief who doesn't wear one. She'd rather kiss ninety times the boy they say she loves than be caught.

When the squatting children (police and thieves as one) bend over a whirling bottle and yell her name, she chooses to tell the truth instead of performing the ninety-time kissing of these fat lips. She says whom she loves.

Her love puts the bottle to his lips and plays it until it chimes like an old train. She doesn't know if it means he loves her too. He probably doesn't, because she has a flat chest.

She will go home alone, devour a muffin and think she should have kissed the one they say she loves.

IV

As she puts down her book *The Brilliant Five* at the hospital's waiting room, a boy approaches her. He is exactly the way boys should be. A spark glints in his coal-dark eyes, and his hair is the color of vanilla cookies.

He accompanies her to her father's bed, and then takes her home, where he climbs into her bed. She takes his hand and lifts her face for a kiss. They remain embraced for hours.

Back from the hospital another day, they go swimming and snuggling in the sea, then melt into one another under a blazingly hot sun. Nobody else sees him, nor will they.

V

The two girls perform plays on stage, ride horses and study the boys at the kibbutz's camp. A tall boy studies the red-haired one back, and that afternoon the two kiss.

They tell the other girl that she needs a boyfriend, and they ask who has eyes for her. Her solitude sticks out like a hump.

She has a blond pigtail and is short, so they find her a short, blonde boy, who shows her the airplane models he builds. She doesn't know what to say to him, and he doesn't say much either. They are glued to the happy couple like parasites.

She asks the boy to meet her again, in order to break up face to face. He says he'll come but doesn't show up. She will hurt for not knowing who dumped whom, for a long time.

VI

The older boy, who lives two floors above hers, is even more beautiful than Jon Bon Jovi.

He breaks a toothy blue-eyed smile when she comes to baby-sit his little sister, then he grabs a piece of torte and leaves. She imagines him in adventurous places with exciting people where she wishes to be, as she makes cheese sandwiches with catsup.

His little sister pulls at their pregnant cat's tail, so the girl releases her grip. The sister cries sorely.

The girl only returns to see the cat giving birth, and also, if she dares, talk to the boy. But he isn't at home. His mother tells her that he's out with the older, pregnant nurse he will marry. He always does the right thing.

The girl thinks about his other woman's baby as she chooses a playful gray kitten to raise.

VII

The inaccessible boy's young brother tells her she is pretty and asks her out. She bears in mind the brothers' family resemblance, although the younger brother's eyes are large and pleading in the lamplight, and not smart and detached. This is the closest she can get.

He reeks of soap and perfume like her father used to smell after taking a shower. She says yes.

The girl's mother gives them her rare blessings, because his eyes adore and admire the girl. Glucose drips into the mother's veins at the hospital, as she explains that a boy who loves a little will not love more over time. It's a mere myth. Her husband, the girl's father, has passed away instead of waiting for her.

The girl will try, but will leave the young brother after three weeks.

VIII

The girl's great grandmother, a friend's mother and an uncle, all tell the girl they want to be children again.

The girl thinks about it when a boy from her class hits her stomach with his powerful fists. He wanted her ball and she refused him.

She collapses to the ground like a noodle in boiling water. Red and black cars race in the air above her. She is unable to scream, lacking air and strength. When she can finally breathe, she aims her sharpened tongue at his softest spots, the way he hit hers. He hates the mention of his retarded brother. The girl fires words.

The boy who loves her will come to rescue her, but it will be too late.

IX

The girl believes that the curly-haired guitar boy will love her, if only the other girls, her best friend included, stopped flirting with him, if only he stayed up with her for the fourth night, if only she deepened the conversation until their minds mixed like grains of sand.

He is the only thing and everything she needs, this is how she loves him.

He has love for her, she knows, but it is not as large as he is, or as is his space within her. It's a crumbling biscuit.

She shoos away the other girls, fights with her best friend, crosses out of the conversation any gossip, and plans to discuss the cosmos.

In the fourth night he plays for a big circle, "God bless the child that's got his own."

And the girl? She is not final.

X

It's in her hands now. If she threw the marble stone to the third chalked-drawn square, skipped the first two squares and jumped on one leg into the third, right beside the stone, then the boy with the funny accent and the serious eyes, the one who brought brownies for lunch, would notice her.

Love signs or swears don't work, she has found, but challenging herself can commit others like magic.

Here he is in the Indian clothes nobody else wears yet, a wanted pirate without a patch or a wooden leg, caught turning his gaze at her.

Here she is, landing in the middle of the third square, glowing in her first accomplished love.

UNLESS

He translated his name from Wolf to Zeev, like opening a dictionary for the local Israelis to understand him. He didn't believe in numerology or astrology, but names worked miracles.

His cat's personality, for instance, its fears, could be traced back to its name, Kishta, slang for "go away!"

He also noticed that every Lillian he ran into was cheerful and warm, and every Ron was lost and searching.

So, with the certainty of an unflappable tie between name and personality, Wolf, now Zeev, searched for a new pack in his new land. He'd left the snow for the desert wind, and it dried his breath and flesh. But he thought there must be someone else, somewhere.

One day, in October, I ran into him near a dwindling stream of mountain water. He seemed to be wounded or sick.

I stopped in my track and sniffed at him. A bitten wolf is dangerous. Unless you are like him. Unless you are like me.

ALL OF THEM

Serving tables was not as hard as dealing with men, especially the café owner, the boss, the man who never apologized.

I hurried back and forth among clients and listened to the background music the radio played between news flashes. The growing tension around the country borders did not concern me as much as the slow kitchen.

During my time off, I saw Ioram, a red-haired, freckled law student with an air of a reliable man. He appeared on my doorstep every evening, but never asked me out or tried to kiss me. He had a vulnerable smile, and sometimes he started saying something and stopped before it came out. I wasn't sure what he wanted.

My girlfriends didn't think much of him, but they did consider Ofer, a dark, tall, advanced law student, an attractive man. When he asked me out, I invited him for coffee, acting upon their admiration alone, still thinking he lacked spark.

Usually, I looked down on law students, since most of them didn't show enough individuality, or because I was one. But the lack of uniqueness wasn't Fon's case. His nickname, Fon, was a part of his last name, and it fit him like a title. On his T-shirt, he wore a pin designed as a marijuana leaf, as if he hadn't been in the legal system's faculty. His blond hair was short and his skinny body was fit, and he used his deep voice on every occasion to perform the clear memory he had of everything he had ever read. He showed disdain for most people, but the few he liked he embraced with his special sparkling smile.

Fon wanted me to live with him as a friend or to be his girlfriend, either one; he was not a passionate man. I might have accepted one offer or the other, had he not completely misread me. He considered me a safe island of logic and tenderness, while I was filled with self-loathing and a desire to rip the world apart. He did not hide the fact he was bisexual, and for that reason I also declined his invitation for wild sex.

***

The evening Ofer, my girl friends' idol, came to my small room at the students' dorms for coffee, Fon arrived as well.

83

He, too, considered Ofer attractive.

I put the kettle on, when, the way coincidences often happen, Ioram hit the doorbell, looked in and headed to my room.

The doorbell rang again. Holding a tray with four mugs of coffee, I somehow managed to open the door for an army officer. Ioram's roommate had told him he could find Ioram at my place, he explained.

Ioram was sitting on my bed, Ofer was scrutinizing my messy room, and Fon was gazing at Ofer's butt, when I let the officer in. He delivered Ioram a recruit letter for a war we didn't expect or wished. We did not know what to say to each other.

Later that night, I spilled hot coffee on the greedy café owner. He found it an adequate opportunity to tell me he knew I had all my tips saved, instead of delivering them to him for a fair sharing. It was true, except the word "fair," so I took my leave.

Ofer and Fon became friends or perhaps lovers, always spending their free time together. Ioram never came back from that war.

My evenings became long and empty.

THE ONE THING THAT MATTERED

They gathered out in nature for a vacation in time where they had camped often.

Behind the shacks, stray cats sneaked into the toilets. The friends had learned to ignore them, the way they avoided anything they couldn't embrace. What they couldn't ignore they forgot soon thereafter.

Their memories floated in and out like a deep breathing, like smoke. They drank until every one of them looked similar and everything about each of them seemed the same.

But one thing still mattered, they were certain, though they couldn't put their fingers on it. It hung over them, then covered the sky.

GONE

The horse is dead, and there's no manure behind the gym.

Your shirt is black with rough metal buttons, yes it is. Our friends from the back-of-the-gym days have split between clean-cut hair and skeletal bodies in designers' clothes. Not you.

Come. Let's go behind the gym for your stolen smoke. I won't take the cigarette out of your mouth, I promise.

Play on my ribs and count my vertebras. Your tongue I remember. Hover over my neck and hum at me. I've been waiting. Hear the sigh of my skin. Play your music, and I'll listen.

My fingers are at your chin and bristles, they are in the grainy ground. Your memory spreads like a net. Cold creeps in.

REUNION

Until the day I received an email from my first boyfriend, I resisted all invitations to any school or scout reunion. Only a few friends had survived my childhood. I didn't expect anyone else to like me that long.

Besides, a reunion is like a remake of a good film: what's the point?

My first boyfriend said he had missed me, and reminded me of everything we had in common. We were short and blonde when we dated at the age of twelve.

I was still short and blonde, though in my thirties. He, I soon learned, was no longer blond, but still short.

He wrote "short" in happy, bold letters. Notwithstanding, he was organizing our scout-tribe's reunion, and I must attend it, he said, since my absence would destroy the event for him and for the other hundred.

The suggestion to meet him and them, the tough and lively, idealistic friends of my youth, twenty years later, was as tempting as having a close look at a magnifying mirror in your late thirties when wrinkles cannot be mistaken for sleeping marks.

I hid behind the regular barricades: children, husband, location, but he had never taken "no" for an answer, and he hadn't changed much. Nor did I. He convinced me.

***

The following two months transformed me into a slimmer, fitter, and blonder version of myself. Still, I observed my mirror reflection, my laugh lines and softening breasts as barriers I should cross before meeting anyone. My husband said I was beautiful, but he loves reunions and doesn't acknowledge the passage of time.

From the unstoppable stream of emails I learned about everybody's lives. I considered the way I should introduce my own story.

***

The folkloric music indicated the meeting place inside the park. As I approached it, two long wooden tables loaded with sandwiches and juice cans appeared on the grass like a flashback from my past.

"You look great!" I told a gaunt, dark man whom I thought was someone named Uri. He turned out to be a passerby.

"Hey! I am so glad you've made it," someone cried, already hugging me against his warm round belly and bare arms. I distanced myself from him enough to look at him and find my old boyfriend's smiling face.

"You look great!" I said, because I did not know what to say. I couldn't tell if he believed me.

Two women approached us.

"You look wonderful!" they told me.

We were not as cruel and sincere as we used to be.

"What do you do?" the former running champion asked me.

"This and that. Writing. You?"

"This is great!" she said.

Making ourselves happy was simple and painless. We liked each other much more now than then.

A pretty woman tapped on my shoulder. She used to master subtle signs of superiority when we competed over the same boys.

"I heard you're a teacher. That's wonderful," I said.

She studied me, the way kids examine a magician when they realize it's all about speed. To my relief, my old boyfriend soon joined us, bringing juice in plastic cups. I sipped and looked around me. Three couples spread over the rocks at the edge of the large lawn. I had no idea those old sweethearts married each other.

My old boyfriend explained none of them did. They were holding hands or sitting with their shoulders touching. Their minds ran a film of a different life and better choices.

I had a sandwich and two more people hugged me. Then I made some other people happy. I felt beautiful and loved. I wished we knew how easy it was twenty years earlier. But maybe we didn't need a good word and a warm embrace at the time.

We surrendered like limestone to the weight of the years. The acute differences lost their sharp edges, and what set us apart melted into round and welcoming sitting corners. In the transformation, all of us became intimate like old lovers. Together, we forgave the years.

"You're more attractive now than then," someone's old boyfriend was saying. I smiled at the beauty of the night, acknowledging the worth of reunions. Then he slipped her a note with his phone number, right under his wife's nose.

MINES

The window divides the night from the blue light, and the glass door separates everything from the only.

You won't be able to talk about it. What you show is what you are to others.

When friends share intimate facts, you wonder if it's a way of manipulation.

They portray themselves, while you let others guess. In the end, it's similar. They are more provocative than you are, but their openness is subjective. As always, the listener dictates the story.

You are hiding between random explosions of truths.

Come on, it's you. You convince yourself. Go wild. But to a point: just don't say too much. Words blow off. As do mines.

(One mine exploded under the foot of a beautiful boy from the U.S. during the university trip. He later said he wasn't angry. Not at the time. But sometime between then and now, he must have been.)

You want, you crave: there must be a further, deeper, grander, exciting emotion.

Now, a recovered man, he makes monkey faces on your screen. A murderer of doubts, he lures you, a turtle, out of your shell, naked and happy and comfortable.

Another year comes and you serve him tea and cheese with carrots. He boils your body and has you for lunch. You are either expanding or fooling yourself.

The day after is melancholic.

THE BISON

It was not until the incident with the bison that Sara
Frishman started eating olives. Green, black, all kinds of
olives, even imported ones. The bitter flesh rolled on her
tongue like Arabic letters.

As soon as Ruben and the children left, she sat on the
pile of planks in the backyard, sucking on olives, licking
their slick brown skin.

When the neighbor's baby cried, ever so loud, her
tongue coiled in, and she held her breath, imagining the
diaper's stench. She could smell it through the sweet aroma
of the over-ripe dates falling off the tree. The air wraps a
transparent layer over pregnant women, letting nothing out.

If she had inhaled that other day, the scent of the
shepherd's sweat would have reached her, and her palms
would have become wet.

The rough seed fell out of her lips before she took
another olive.

She had never seen a bison in her life. It had a huge

erection. She stared at it while the shepherd stood behind her, talking in Arabic.

He could have said anything. She barely felt the rhythm of the words, the languishing end, and she didn't turn around. It had been long since words played with her body like that.

She put another olive in her mouth.

That day, she found she was pregnant. The baby was Ruben's, but she felt it could have been the shepherd's.

A wagtail landed on the palm tree, and a date fell on the ground, already rotten.

FIRE. WATER.

The son flies an airplane over the handrail. The daughter
yells she won't wash her hair. The son throws a bomb at her,
into the living room. The daughter looks for the electric
heater. The mother washes the dishes as if the wars were over
now. The father walks the dog outside.

The son rides the mezzanine's half wall. The daughter
says she will die, because the day is too cold for a shower.
The son, he slips down the handrail, a small skate in his
hands. The daughter, she carries the heater to the bathroom.
The son piles blankets by the bathroom to build a barricade.
The mother washes dishes in the kitchen. The father walks
the dog outside.

The son kicks the bathroom door open. The daughter
screams she is cold. The son sends the skate into the
bathroom. The daughter drags one blanket inside. The son
looks at the bathroom mirror. The daughter is naked. The
son laughs out loud. The mother washes dishes. The father
walks the dog outside.

The daughter shouts she'll show around the picture with the son's butt out. The son dives onto the floor for his skate and his jet. The daughter cries he should not see her. The son turns on the water to fly his jet through waterfalls. The daughter shows the finger to the son. The son throws his skate at the daughter. The daughter shouts, "Mother! Father!" The mother washes dishes. The father walks the dog outside.

The son jumps up and down like a monkey. The daughter leaps at the son. The son bumps into the electric heater, and he and the heater fall down. The daughter throws the blanket at him. The son gets up and covers her head with the blanket. The daughter says she is warm and good. The son pushes the daughter at the water. The daughter falls over the heater with the blanket over her head. The son drops the jet, the bombs, the skate and pulls her from the heater. The blanket's hem turns black. The mother washes the dishes. The father walks the dog outside.

The daughter falls. The son pulls. The daughter rises. Falls. Rises. Throws. Pulls. The son. The daughter. The electric heater. The water in the shower. Fire. Water. The mother washes the dishes. The father walks the dog outside.

96

A NARROW BRIDGE

I've sung this ancient song in those moments my mouth started singing and I listened with interest to what would come out of it.

"The whole world is nothing but a narrow bridge, a narrow bridge, a narrow bridge."

It's so narrow, my back yard is bigger.

My children are playing in it, in and out of a blue plastic basin. They have been laughing but now they are fierce as they always are in their disputes against one another and for each other when the neighbors' children threaten one of them. Their shouts are so piercing it's a miracle their tiny bodies are capable of producing them.

I almost step out, but the wrath dissolves at once as the cookie in question drops from their hands into the water. They stand side by side to observe it as it sinks. When it's completely sunk, they fish it out, split wet bits between them, test and taste it like scientists at work.

And then the air freezes and explodes with noise, smoke

and fire. A field behind the house is burning. Every dispute has two sides, I know. I care about mine now. My kids are in danger.

***

My body produces fiercer shouts than theirs as I gather them in my arms, checking they are fine, although the explosion was not in my backyard.

They are screaming, so I calm down. I sing for them:

"The whole world is nothing but a narrow bridge, a narrow bridge, a narrow bridge.

The most important thing is to never fear, never fear, never fear."

SUNNY

It looks like nothing bad can happen. The day is cloudless, inviting outside in the tender way of autumn. The trail to the beach is still swamped from last week's rain. Thirty people could lie in the rain-pool but only seven do. Other pools spread around them and among the dunes in tones of blue, green and bronze.

She knows it's The Holocaust Memorial Day, one of many. For days going on years she has carried her memories of them, parents who were surprised by her presence every day until they passed away. Their own memories were heavy with their memories of their families, the dead families in Poland and Austria, lost to war. She carries heavy memories full of holes. They are nestled inside her, but sunny days like this one push them aside.

There haven't been enough good moments this year. She's thought again and again—she always thinks—that she'd be alone again, if not immediately, then in a few years, and if nobody left her or the place or the time or this life, she'd get old no matter how much she'd resist it, and she does put a fight.

But now, they follow the trail, the seven of them. One couple has brought a poodle whose teeth go upward over its mouth. Another couple brought an adolescent daughter lonely enough to join them. The third one brought nothing, only water and a towel.

They splash through knee-high water to an unsteady little bridge and then into the dunes, and their feet leave traces in the sand, like lost traces in the snow, people taken and guarded and beat and sent away on foot in the freezing winter. Her family.

On TV, a film from that past showed the bad days of people going toward their worst day yet. The director procured the most disgusting angles of what the cameramen considered a most disgusting people. Was this my family?

We are going to the beach.

The sun tans the skin to a point before burning, then the breeze blows on it like a mother blowing air on her daughter's wound. Sometime, after the holocaust and after Mom's settling down in Israel, doctors warned that blowing air on a wound involves bacteria and inflammation. But she, a blonde-red-haired woman, with European delicate skin, thin legs, and heavy breasts disciplined by triangular bra cups, she with frayed eyelashes surrounding surprisingly light green eyes looking tired from the years and the length of each day—she knows what's best for her daughter.

She hasn't been "there," though, the mother, not in the ghetto or the camps, not in hell, like the father, the stocky man with a gentle face and darker hair and eyes and skin than his daughter's, and yet his eyes twinkled, they did, much more than the mother's. He would have said that's fine, go out, enjoy yourself today, but light a candle for my parents, and my little brother, and my aunt and uncle, and my cousins, except for the one who escaped, thank goodness. He uses such expressions, but they have no god in them, only heart.

Her mother, too, however, has lost family. She ran away and lost everyone else, except for her daughter, that rough fruit of the desert, who'd become a woman with no explanation, no excuse for her neglect of the dead. Nothing is sustained by her spirit, her soaring spirit in the dunes and the pools and the oceans, nothing to hold onto in days to come but a candle she may or may not light. She goes, and dives, and takes pictures. Nothing bad will happen, not yet, not today.

ABOUT MY LIFE LENGTH

Yesterday, a fortune teller from Jerusalem told me I'd
live until the age of eighty-nine.

I had always believed I'd live until about fifty or sixty at
most, then pass the torch and the worries about tombstones
to those who would outlive me.

The fact is, that after having outlived quite a lot of
people, after surviving grownups who died from cancer and
youngsters who were killed in wars, I made a deal with a
certain entity. The agreement was that nobody I loved could
die before me. In return, I'd keep my faith intact.

Now, if that fortune teller, another queen of secret lands,
was right, and they often are, then a big number of people
will approach or even pass their hundredth birthday, and
this, if they died the day I would. If there weren't any war or
any such apocalypse, they may just go on living even longer.

The fortune teller observed the palm of my hand,
or rather, the corpulent space under my thumb, and
announced she'd have to fight a curse. Apparently, I have a

cursing enemy.

She dug into the many layers of her colorful dress and brought out a buttermilk-colored angel resting on a dirty sunflower. To make it work, she needed a money note, she said, and not the one I had given her as a modest payment for her service.

I resisted. I'd need lots of money if I lived to be eighty-nine. She promised she'd give it back to me after executing the anti-curse spell.

I saw a policeman in front of us, relaxed and gave her a note.

"You feel pain, here, in the sphincter," she said, hitting me hard just below my stomach. "It's time nobody hurts you," she added, and I nodded whole-heartedly.

She rubbed the angel with my money. "Do you believe?" she asked me.

"In what?"

"Do you believe?" she insisted.

I assumed that the password was "yes."

It worked. She hit my shoulders with the sunflower, and asked me to say, "I'm free."

"I'm free."

She smiled, revealing her pink and black gums. "No curse. You are free to go."

"Thank you. Can I have my note, please?" I asked.

"You're abusing. The curse passed to the note," she said.

"I need it."

"You're abusing," she shrieked.

"Give me the note, it's mine."

The fortune teller knew, as she had told me before predicting my life length, that I could get very angry. She handed me my note.

I felt her bitter gaze, as I walked to my car, contemplating the future. Where would all these old people live? Will my beloved ones found a community for the outliving? Will they remember me?

I used the note at the gas station. If it had been cursed, I'd have to die on the hills on my way home. But if the prediction prevailed, I wouldn't die until I was eighty-nine.

I arrived home, with a whole of a lot of future. During lunch I saw all my family, lined and bent but smiling, a hundred years old.

ACKNOWLEDGEMENTS

In memory of my beloved parents, Frieda and Shimon Grubstein, my aunt, Miriam Hammel, who passed some writing genes forward, my dear cousin, Gady, Uncle Yaacov, and my good friend, Bob Krawetz, who generously offered his editing skills when I started writing in English.

I am grateful for the professional, intellectual and emotional support of my friends in the Hot Pants Room and A Hell of a Universe (Vacancies), and the Zoetrope work and fun ambience.

This collection carries my love to my husband, Pablo, my daughter, Noa, and my son, Tom, the family whose love and humor sustains not only my writing but my life.

AUTHOR'S NOTE

A winner of prestigious awards such as Margaret Atwood Studies Magazine Prize, The Hawthorne Citation Contest, and Iowa Fiction Award's finalist, Avital Gad-Cykman's work has been widely published online and in print, including *The Literary Review*, *Glimmer Train*, *McSweeney's Quarterly*, and *Michigan Quarterly Review*, with work upcoming in *CALYX Journal*. Her stories can also be found in many anthologies, among them the new W.W. Norton's *Flash Fiction International Anthology*. Born and raised in Israel, she now resides with her family on an island in Brazil.